The PUPPY Who Needed a FRIEND

Tracey Herrold

Illustrated by Bill Robison

To Emily

Published by Willowisp Press, Inc.
401 E. Wilson Bridge Road, Worthington, Ohio 43085

Copyright © 1989 by Willowisp Press, Inc.

Printed in the United States of America   10 9 8 7 6 5 4 3 2 1   ISBN 0-87406-396-5

Basil was a sad-eyed little basset hound, with long ears and a big roly-poly tummy. Some people might think Basil was a funny-looking puppy, but not Basil's special playmate. She was his best friend!

Basil liked nothing better than to play all day with his playmate. After he was all tired out, Basil loved to curl up on her lap for a very long nap.

One morning, Basil's playmate was gone for a long time. Basil couldn't wait for her to come home so they could play outside together. But when his playmate came home, she had a new friend with her. It was a tiny kitten.

Basil's playmate spent all afternoon playing with her kitten. She ran around outside with her new kitten and even fed it special treats. She didn't seem to have any time at all to play with Basil.

Who will I play with now? wondered Basil as he sadly slunk away.

Basil looked down toward the garden and saw a little bunny sitting in the middle of it. The bunny was busy munching on a bunch of carrots.

Oh, boy! Maybe that little bunny will play with me, Basil thought as he scampered happily toward the garden.

The little bunny took one look at Basil, and its eyes grew big with fear. The bunny stopped eating, and quickly hopped away.

Maybe the bunny wants to play chase, Basil thought. So, Basil took off and chased after the bunny. They ran around and around, until the bunny disappeared down a hole in the ground. Basil was running so fast that he didn't even see the hole.

KER-FLOP! Before he knew it, Basil's big feet had tripped over the hole. He lay flat on his face.

Basil sadly picked himself up off the ground. Boy, thought Basil. First my playmate doesn't want to play with me. And now the bunny doesn't want to be my friend, either!

Just then, Basil heard a crackling noise in the leaves. A tiny squirrel poked its head out. Hey! Maybe the squirrel will be my friend, Basil thought. Now I'll have someone to play with.

The squirrel stood still for a moment and took a long look at Basil. Then the squirrel dashed into a hollow log that was nearby.

Maybe the squirrel wants to play hide and seek, thought Basil cheerfully. Basil tried to dive inside the hollow log, too, but his tummy was too round. His tummy stopped him from finding the squirrel. Even worse, Basil was stuck!

Basil pushed and pulled, and pushed and pulled. He tried and tried, but his roly-poly tummy was stuck. Finally, with one big push, there was a huge KER-FLOP! Basil had pushed himself free at last.

Basil picked himself up and walked sadly away. Gee, thought Basil. First my playmate wouldn't be my friend. Then the bunny and the squirrel ran away and wouldn't play with me, either!

Just then, Basil heard a rustling sound. He saw a raccoon up ahead eating berries off a vine. Hey! Basil thought. I bet that raccoon will play with me. Basil bounded toward the raccoon.

But when the raccoon saw Basil, its eyes grew big with fear. It scurried up a nearby tree as fast as it could.

Maybe the raccoon wants to play follow the leader, Basil thought. So, Basil jumped and jumped, trying to climb the tree, too.

Basil tried and tried to climb the tree. He jumped so high that he lost his balance.

KER-FLOP! KER-FLOP! KER-FLOP! Basil tumbled over and over, his long ears flying over his head. He finally landed flat on his little brown back with a great big KER-PLOP!

Basil was tired. He didn't want to play anymore. All he wanted was to curl up in his playmate's lap and take a good long nap.

Up ahead, Basil saw his playmate. And her little kitten was sitting happily in her lap.

It's just not fair, Basil thought sadly. That kitten is taking a nap where I should be. I don't have any friends. A big tear trickled down Basil's cheek as he walked away.

Suddenly, Basil heard his playmate's voice.

"Basil, Basil," she called. "Where have you been? We've been looking all over for you!"

Looking for me? Basil wondered. Why would she have been looking for me? Oh, boy! Maybe she wants to be my friend again! Basil thought and hurried toward her.

"There's room on my lap for both of you to take a nap!" Basil's playmate said. "And when you wake up, we can all play a game!"

Basil wagged his tail happily and climbed into his playmate's lap. Basil was glad to have his playmate back. And now, thought Basil, I not only have one friend. I have two!